This paperback edition first published in 2018 by Andersen Press Ltd.

First published in Great Britain in 2001 by Andersen Press Ltd.,

20 Vauxhall Bridge Road, London SW1V 2SA

Text and Illustration copyright © Tony Ross, 2001

Colour separated in Switzerland by Photolitho AG, Zürich.

Printed and bound in Malaysia.

1 3 5 7 9 10 8 6 4 2

British Library Cataloguing in Publication Data available.

ISBN 978 1 78344 633 9

Little Princess

THIS BOOK BELONGS TO

_____

Little Princess

I Want My Dummy!

Tony Ross

Andersen Press

"I want my dummy!"

"You're not still using a dummy?" said the Admiral.
"It's nice!" said the Little Princess.

"This tastes much better than a dummy," said the Cook.
"No, it doesn't!" said the Little Princess.

"Where's my dummy gone?"

"... I want my dummy!"

"How did it get up the chimney?"

"I'll never lose it again!"

"Where's my dummy? I want my dummy!"

"What's it doing under the dog?" said the Little Princess.

"I'll NEVER lose my dummy again!" she said.

"NEVER, never, never, never..."

"Burglars have taken my dummy! I want my dummy!"

"How did it get into the dustbin?"

"It tastes better after a wash!" said the Little Princess.

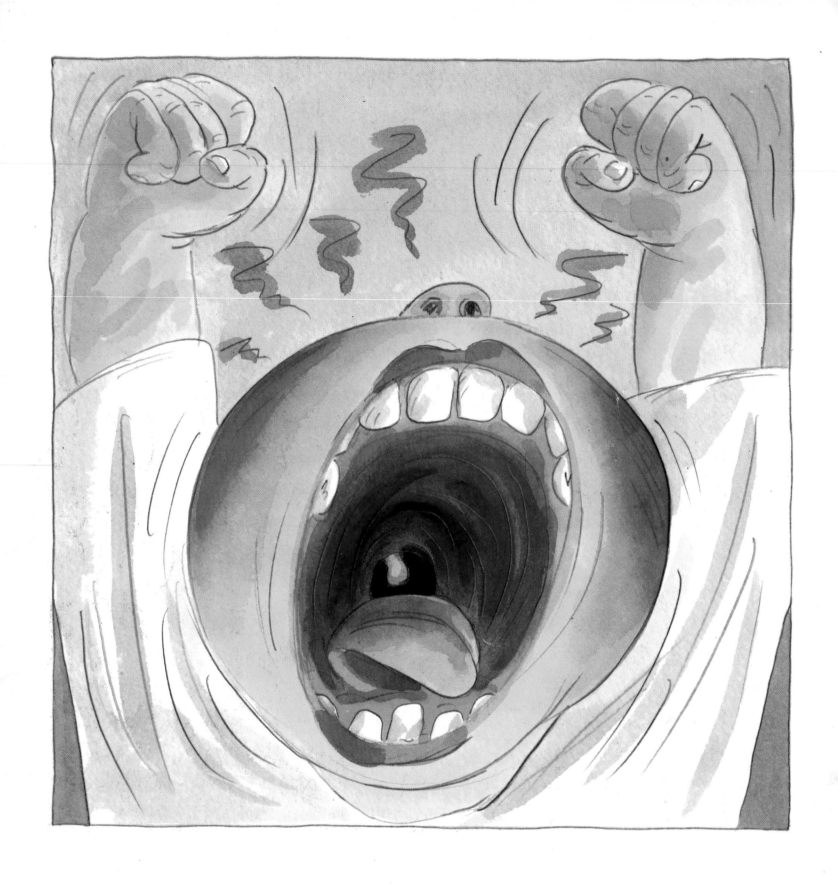

"It's gone again! I WANT MY DUMMY!"

"How did it get into the pond?"

"I'll never let it go again!" said the Little Princess.
"It's safe on this ribbon."

"Aren't you too grown-up for a dummy?" said the Prime Minister.
"No!" said the Little Princess.

"Soldiers don't have dummies!" said the General.
"Ladies don't have dummies, either," said the Maid.

"Well I do, SO THERE!" said the Little Princess.

"That dummy looks stupid!" said her cousin.

"It does!" said the Little Princess.
"But it's not mine..."

"... it's Gilbert's!"